ABOUT THE AUTHOR

Matt Porter was short-listed for the Speech Pathology Book of the Year and is a previous winner of the CYA Writing Conference Competition. His hilarious books and engaging school visits have been a hit from Victoria to Queensland since he burst onto the publishing scene in 2010. Check out his latest news at www.mattporter.com.au

Also by Matt Porter

Mr Sergeant and the Dodgeballs of Doom
Mr Jackpot and the Stash of Cash
Mr Crikey and the Greedy Griffith
Ms Law and the Corn-fusing Case of the Broken Window
Ms Runway and Australia's Next Top Merino
My Country
Picture Perfect

Stephanie Chiocci and the Cooper's Hill Cheese Chase

Matt Porter

FORD ST

Published by Ford Street Publishing, an imprint of
Hybrid Publishers, PO Box 52, Ormond VIC 3204
Melbourne Victoria Australia
© Matt Porter 2018
2 4 6 8 10 9 7 5 3 1

This publication is copyright. Apart from any use as permitted under the Copyright Act 1968, no part may be reproduced by any process without prior written permission from the publisher. Requests and enquiries concerning reproduction should be addressed to
Ford Street Publishing Pty Ltd
162 Hoddle Street, Abbotsford, Vic 3067.
Ford Street website: www.fordstreetpublishing.com

Creator: Porter, Matt 1980– author.
Title: Stephanie Chiocci and the Cooper's Hill Cheese Chase
/ Matt Porter.
ISBN: 9781925272888 (paperback)
Target Audience: For primary school age.
Subjects: football – Juvenile fiction.
Dewey Number: A823.4

Cover design : Cathy Larsen ©
In-house editor: Tim Harris

Printed in Australia by McPherson's Printing Group

Hey everyone

Welcome to my first book! I'm Stephanie Chiocci, or 'Choch', as my teammates call me. Captaining Collingwood's Australian Football League Women's team is an exciting job, and I'm just as excited to be appearing in this book for kids.

Stephanie Chiocci and the Cooper's Hill Cheese Chase sees me jetting off to England and racing down a hill steeper than the grandstands at the MCG to capture a wheel of cheese. But more importantly, I'm helping out a little girl and making sure a bully gets what's coming to him.

You're obviously a huge footy fan, so

you'll definitely love this book. If you also love laughing, action and adventure then you're in for a real treat.

Seeya at the end of the book!

[signature] #17

Steph Chiocci

Chapter 1

'Good old Collingwood forever, they know how to play the game!' my ringtone proudly sings.

Eddie McGuire is calling me. It's the third time today. He may be president of the Collingwood Football Club, and I the captain of the women's team, but this is getting ridiculous.

'Hey, Ed,' I say . . . again.

Eddie's voice crackles through the phone. 'Steph Chiocci! If you're overseas competing in some stupid sporting event, I'll have you sprinting the stairs of the

Holden Centre till next season!'

I peer down the steep slope of Cooper's Hill in England. Tomorrow I'll be hurtling down this hill, chasing after a dinner plate-sized wheel of Double Gloucester cheese, alongside fifty other people. But we're not desperate for cheese. At least, I'm not, anyway. The cheese chase is a race: the Cooper's Hill Cheese-Rolling Race. And I'm here to win it.

'You've got form for disappearing,' says Eddie. 'Last month you posted a selfie while ironing your shirt and abseiling down the Grand Canyon at the Extreme Ironing World Championships. You were really pressing your luck!'

'Next time I enter an Iron Woman contest, I'll read the fine print,' I say. 'But I raised thousands for charity . . . and my Collingwood shirt has never been smoother.'

'The Penguin Herding World Championships are on in Antarctica, but our captain can't mark with frostbitten fingers. Believe it or not, we gave you rest days to rest!'

'Penguin herding, eh?' My voice shows more enthusiasm than is safe for my boss to hear. 'Ahh . . . the only black and white birds I chase are my Magpie teammates at training. You've got nothing to worry about, Ed.'

Eddie's worry isn't unreasonable. An injury could rule me out for the Australian Football League Women's season. Our chances of winning the premiership would suffer. But how could I not come to England after the email I received last week? When Eddie's finally done checking I'm not up to anything that might rule me out for our next game against the Bulldogs, I bring the message up on my phone and re-read it.

Hey Steph

My name's Emily and I'm ten. I watch all your AFLW games online. I'm going to be a footballer when I grow up, just like you. Over here in England my granny makes delicious cheese for a living. But another cheesemaker, Neville O'Shea, is pushing her out of business. Neville also wins the Cooper's Hill Cheese-Rolling Race every year. Any chance you can come over here and beat him for us? I saw your post from halfway down the Grand Canyon and know you're up for a challenge! Neville might force Granny's business to close, but we can beat him in the race.

Please help us
Emily Adams

A stocky, middle-aged man, wearing a flat cap and polo shirt, battles his way up

Cooper's Hill. His red shirt matches the colour of his cheeks.

'This hill's steeper than the grandstand at the MCG,' I say.

Finally scaling the ninety-metre incline, the man introduces himself as Alex Fairbank: Race Director.

Beneath us, the green grass sways in a gentle breeze. Tall trees throw shadows across the slope. No doubt it will be a much wilder scene come race day. Probably a mix between the Western Bulldogs' cheer squad and the MCG toilet queue at half-time.

'Tomorrow you'll roll a wheel of cheese down here, we'll barrel after it, and whoever grabs the cheese first, wins?' I ask.

'Cheese-chasing is no easy task,' replies Alex. 'Racers can suffer concussions or broken bones. Some poor sods get both.'

A wiry man with thick black hair barges

past. The collar of his polo shirt is flipped up, and even though he's the size of a back pocket, he still manages to look down his long nose at us.

'If you'd be so kind as to shove off, cheese-heads, there's testing to be done.'

He plants a yellow peg into the ground, then places a wooden wheel in front of it. Holding the wheel in position with his foot, the man flicks out a notepad and pen.

'Three, two, one, release,' he says to himself. The wheel tumbles down the hill, the man bobbing and leaning the whole time as if he's riding every bump while jotting notes on the wheel's journey.

Rolling into the long grass at the bottom of the hill, the wheel tumbles on its side.

The man speeds after his equipment. Never looking off balance, he descends the slope like a hare, leaping over holes and sidestepping stones with his skinny legs.

'Is that bloke a few slices short of a block of cheese?' I ask.

'No,' mutters Alex.

'Is he a cheese-rolling safety officer?' I doubt such a position exists after the carnage I've seen watching past cheese chases online.

Alex shakes his head sternly. 'That hard-boiled excuse for a human is a dairy producer: cheese, milk, yoghurt . . . He'll be a competitor of yours. He's won the last five races. Five too many. His name's O'Shea.'

'Neville O'Shea,' I say, knowingly.

Alex shoots me a surprised look.

'Word is he's disliked more than an ice bath after a rainy training session,' I explain.

Neville climbs the hill, moves his yellow peg a half-step to the left of his first release spot, and re-rolls his wooden wheel.

I point at his equipment. 'Serious business?'

His eyes dart from the wheel to his notepad and back again. 'By Jove, all business is serious.'

Chapter 2

The inside of the rental car smells of the vanilla air freshener hanging from the rear vision mirror. It's not as comforting as the Deep Heat aroma in the change rooms before a big match, but it's certainly better than the stench of the pile of sweaty footy jumpers afterwards. Emily claps as I step from the car and onto the green grass of her grandmother's front lawn.

'Steph! Thanks so much for coming.' She wraps her arms around me then steps back. 'Wow, your legs are even longer in real life! You're going to smash O'Shea.' She grabs my hand and leads me into the dairy behind her grandmother's house.

Heather Adams hurries along the trench, a slight limp as she moves, and pulls the suction cups from a cow's teats. She huffs a breath, blowing a stray grey hair from her eyes.

'Granny, there's someone here to see you.' Emily bounces as she calls.

Descending into the concrete trench has a similar feel to walking down the race after a game of footy. Of course, the footy race doesn't have twenty cows' bums pointing at you, but it does have opposition fans, who can be just as nasty. 'It's a pleasure to meet you,' I say.

'You're an Aussie?' asks Heather. 'What are you doing all the way over here?'

I give her granddaughter a gentle nudge. 'Emily had a special request.'

Heather shoots her granddaughter a suspicious look.

'I've heard all about you, Heather,' I say. 'Alex Fairbank reckons you make the best Double Gloucester in the world.'

Heather removes the suction cups from another cow.

'Bless Alex's boots. But I need a miracle to keep producing my cheeses. That top-notch toff O'Shea moved into town some years back. His factory has all the bells and whistles, and he can produce triple the cheese I can for half the price. Neville's determined to send me broke, even though he's already minted.'

Fishing around in my pocket, I produce two fifty-pound notes.

Heather yanks a lever, opening the gate at the end of the dairy and allowing the cows to amble into the fresh air. They wander in single file onto the track leading to the paddocks, like footy players following their captain onto the field.

'I don't take charity,' says Heather.

'It's not charity. Charity is ironing shirts for money while dangling halfway down the Grand Canyon. I want to buy a cheese wheel. Double Gloucester, thanks.'

She looks me up and down before turning her attention to the cows on the other side of the dairy. 'You'd be proper sick if you tried to eat nine pounds of cheese. Lovey, what's the real reason you want a wheel?'

'Steph's an elite athlete in Australia. She's entered the Cooper's Hill Cheese-Rolling Race,' says Emily. 'She's going to smash O'Shea for us.'

'That's very nice of you, deary,' says Heather. 'I'd pay proper money to see Neville O'Shea spitting chips when he loses.'

'And as you make the cheese I'll be chasing,' I say, 'I'd like a wheel for training.'

Heather pulls another lever, releasing the cows on the other side of the trench. Her smile vanishes. 'Not many folks know that anymore. In years past my cheese would be seen in the winner's hands in newspapers around the world. But since that snake-in-the-grass showed up, he's always covered up my logo in the winner's photo.'

'Steph will make sure your cheese is front and centre when she wins,' says Emily.

'Like Eddie in our team photo,' I add.

'I truly hope so.' Heather rushes past us to refill the feed buckets with hay. 'But don't waste your hard-earned here. The winner keeps the cheese from the race.'

I've spent years studying for games of footy. I was knee-high to a ruckwoman when I started learning the game. It's important to know who the opposition's best player is, how they set up in the forward line and how their oval plays. Practising with the official cheese could be the difference between me winning or face-planting halfway down Cooper's Hill.

'I have to train with the official cheese,' I explain, helping Heather fill the feed buckets. 'My coaches always say failing to prepare is preparing to fail.'

'A cheese-rolling coach?' Heather laughs as she herds in a new batch of cows. 'Most racers just charge down the hill and hope to be in one piece at the bottom.'

I allow my mind to wander, imagining a coach barking cheese-rolling orders instead of footy tactics. 'Get the cheese into the corridor! We're getting thrashed in the hard cheese-gets! Any chance of someone picking up O'Shea!?'

I snap out of it. 'Aussie Rules is my game. I have a footy coach, but he . . .

he doesn't know I'm here. Neither does the club president. In fact, the club president's head may explode if he learns about the race.'

Heather winks. 'Your secret's safe with me, love.' She disappears momentarily and returns with an apricot-coloured cheese wheel about the size of a car's steering wheel.

My legs wobble under the weight as I accept the cheese. Pinching my fifty-pound notes between my fingers, I push the money forwards.

Heather grabs a set of suction cups from the trench instead. 'Beat that nit-wit Neville, win the race, and the cheese is on me.'

'Deal!' Emily calls before I can reply. 'Granny, your cheese will be on the front page of every newspaper from Gloucester to Collingwood.'

'I hope so. But where's Collingwood?'

'It's my home turf,' I reply. 'They love their footy down that way . . . and their cheese.'

Chapter 3

Some players spend their rest days on the couch. Others play video games. I'm lugging a four-kilogram dairy product up a hill that's higher than the roof of the Holden Centre.

I drop the bulky cheese wheel from my shoulder as Emily and I reach the top of Cooper's Hill.

Thwack!

The cheese thumps into the turf, leaving a dent in the dirt.

'Remind me not to volunteer to chair off the first player to reach a hundred games,' I say.

Emily places her hand on top of the rounded edge of the cheese. 'You ready, Steph? You're so going to thrash O'Shea.'

I pull my ponytail tight, ensuring my hair will stay out of my eyes, take three deep breaths, then nod.

Lifting her hand, Emily counts as the cheese begins tumbling down the hill. 'One . . . two . . .'

The cheese wheel quickly gathers speed. Flicking up clumps of dirt and blades of grass, it zooms down the slope.

'Three . . . go!'

I shoot down the hill.

Striding with my long legs, I quickly make ground on the wheel.

I've always been confident below my knees on the footy field. Once I catch up to the cheese I'll be able to scoop it up with clean hands, just like crumbing a pack in Collingwood's back line. But instead of then having to fend off the full forward, baulk two others and pinpoint a pass to a midfielder, the hard work will already be done. Just grabbing the cheese wheel will make me the champion cheese-chaser on race day and score a win for Emily and Heather.

I race behind the Double Gloucester, bend low and stretch my arms towards the target.

Zip!

Hitting the steepest part of the slope, the cheese speeds away from my grasp.

'Eddie would have me dragged for that!' I call.

'You can do it, Steph!' calls Emily.

'Get back here!' I don't normally talk to food, but now seems like a good time to start.

I push into top gear, but even my top speed isn't enough.

The cheese wheel races across the flat stretch of ground at the bottom of the hill and into the long grass.

Panting and red-faced, I throw my hands behind my head. 'Now I know how my opponents feel!'

Back at the top of the hill, I plonk on the ground next to the cheese wheel.

'You'll get it next time,' says Emily. 'I know you will.'

'If I'm going to get it, I need a new tactic,' I say.

During preseason at Collingwood, we learned visualisation. A guru guided us, teaching us to picture in our minds what we want to achieve and how we're going to do it. Before every set shot at goal I visualise my foot kicking through the ball and the footy sailing between the big sticks. Sometimes I then picture the ball flying into the crowd and falconing an opposition supporter who's been heckling me, but that's another story. 'If you can't see it happening, it won't happen', as Eddie always says.

Gripping the cheese wheel, I visualise it as something I've caught thousands of times before: a footy. I imagine the cheese wheel has red, shiny leather with black stitching. I picture it divided into four segments, with two pointy ends. Putting my nose forward, I even give it a sniff and try to imagine the leathery smell that wafts from every new footy.

'Pwoah!' The cheese smell is too powerful to ignore. 'I'll just visualise, not sniffualise.'

Emily grabs the Double Gloucester and rolls it down the hill.

In my mind, it is a red ball, bouncing

down the hill at the park across the street from my childhood home in Carlton.

'One . . . two . . .' counts Emily.

This time I don't wait for three. Dashing towards the cheese wheel, I take up position behind it.

The cheese bobbles over a bump.

I bend even lower this time, like a ruckwoman who's had the ball kicked at her bootlaces.

Amongst the green grass, daisies and clumps of dirt that I dash past, I notice a small ledge sticking out from the hill up ahead. The cheese will bounce up off the ledge! And when it does, I'll be able to snatch it at hip height.

Three steps from the ledge. I straighten my back.

Two steps away. I stretch my arms forward.

One step. I spread my fingers.

The cheese hits the ledge.

My eyes focus on the target, ready to snatch the cheese as soon as it bobs up.

Zip!

Instead of springing up like a centre bounce, the cheese shoots off the ledge at ankle height, like a worm-burning drop punt.

Slap!

My hands slap together, totally missing the Double Gloucester.

'And you're Collingwood's captain? The other players must be truly hopeless,' yells a familiar voice from the base of the hill. Neville O'Shea has obviously been researching the hill layout *and* me. The tiny troublemaker watches the cheese roll in front of his feet and disappear into the long grass, making no attempt to stop it.

'Drop your shoulder, Steph!' calls Emily. 'Run through him!'

While Emily's suggestion is tempting, I ignore it. Anyway, by the look of her red face and pose, it seems as if she might bolt down the hill and flatten Neville herself. I throw my hands behind my head and suck in several quick breaths at the bottom of the hill.

'Give Australia a bell, would you? Ask them to send some real competition,' sneers Neville. 'Because beating you will be a piece of cake. Or should I say a cakewalk?' He begins singing, out of tune, Collingwood's club song. 'Oh, the cheese chase is a cakewalk, for the good old Nev O'Shea!'

Chapter 4

Emily and I enter Heather's kitchen, a footy tucked under my arm.

Heather notices the glum look on my face. 'You've got a face like a wet weekend. What's wrong?'

'Even if she catches up to the cheese, she can't pick where it'll roll,' says Emily. 'But she'll get it. We can't let Neville win.'

'Why don't you train with something you're used to, like that Aussie Rules ball?'

I spin the ball in my hand as I speak. 'I tried. But when I visualised the cheese as a footy, I misread the bounce.'

'Here's the thing, there's no time for visualising when you're racing down Cooper's Hill. The local bobby recorded my Double Gloucester speeding downhill at over forty miles an hour.'

I calculate the speed. 'That's over sixty kilometres an hour!'

'Try chasing a *real* football.'

I was taught to train as if I were playing. Would chasing a footy downhill prepare me for racing after the cheese wheel? 'Do you reckon it'll help?'

A grin flashes on Emily's face. 'I've got it!' She cups her hand over her mouth and whispers into her grandmother's ear.

Heather's eyes light up. 'It'll take some work, but it's a fabulous idea.'

Emily ushers me to the door. 'Practise chasing that footy down the hill. Granny and I have work to do.' And with that, they disappear into the cheese-making room.

Before long I'm back atop Cooper's Hill, ball in hand.

'Good old Collingwood forever!' my ringtone sings.

'An ad popped up on my computer for an Avalanche Run in Alaska,' says Eddie. 'Being trapped under tonnes of snow will be the least of your worries if I find out you're there!'

'No snow here, Chief. I'm about to do some ball work.'

'Good. I want you burying three forwards, not buried under three metres of snow. But don't overdo the ball work. We need you fresh for the Bulldogs next weekend.'

I'll be fresh for the Bulldogs all right . . . fresh off a victory in the Cooper's Hill Cheese-Rolling Race, but there's no way

I'm going to tell Eddie that.

I hang up the phone and balance the footy on its point.

'Frightfully sorry to interrupt your so-called training, but why don't you start with something you have a hope of catching?' Neville drops a tiny circle of cheese, the size of a twenty-cent coin, on the ground.

Somehow, I resist the urge to point out that if cheese wheels were made to scale, the one next to me would be perfect for my tiny tormentor. Years of having full-forwards trying to put me off my game have taught me that responding only gives them motivation to keep yapping.

Neville plunges his hands into his kitbag and carefully organises his gear on the grass: a tape measure, pens, wooden wheel, ice pack, bandages and even a small shovel.

He carries more gear to cheese-chasing training than I take to a game of footy. In fact, he's got more gear than I'd take on a month-long holiday!

I release the only equipment I brought to training: my footy.

The ball bobbles down the hill, gathering speed with every bounce.

Just as I expect, the footy bounces high when it lands on its side and shoots forward after hitting the ground near its point.

'That's more like it!' I cheer. Great, now I'm talking to food *and* sports equipment.

I bolt after the ball, my long arms pumping. Running downhill isn't as strenuous as the hill sprints we sweated through during preseason, but the danger level is multiplied by a hundred. Any false step could see me roll an ankle, or worse.

And the injuries from the hill would be nothing compared to the lecture I'd cop from Eddie.

The ledge halfway down the hill looms again. But this time I'm chasing a footy; I know I'll be able to read the bounce.

Zip!

Instead of bending down to scoop up the footy, I dash straight past it. Stopping metres in front of the ball, I spin and ready my hands at chest height for the mark.

The ball bounces on the ledge and darts forward, just like the cheese wheel, and into my waiting mitts. I hold the ball above my head like I'm claiming a mark.

Neville wanders down the hill, poking at sections of turf with his foot. 'It seems Cooper's Hill delivers the ball better than your Collingwood teammates. I might have reason to be concerned . . . if it was a football we were to chase tomorrow.

But the Double Gloucester is a difficult pursuit. It has a tendency to bounce up at some times and speed away at others.'

I continue to ignore Neville, but I know he's right. If it were a competition that required height, strength or stamina, he'd be copping the wooden spoon. But as long as we're chasing a cheese wheel, he will have an advantage.

'May the best racer win,' I say.

'Thanks,' replies Neville. 'I intend to.'

Chapter 5

Game day! I tear off the sheets and leap out of bed.

While it isn't actually 'game day', I have the same feelings as before a big game of footy: butterflies fly around in my stomach, my legs feel like pistons ready to pump, and the sense of what's going to happen, like waking up on Christmas morning, buzzes around my brain.

Slipping on my black Collingwood shorts and a Magpies polo top I begin my preparations. Stretching against the kitchen wall, I close my eyes and form a visual image of myself chasing the cheese wheel down Cooper's Hill. My feet land steadily on the turf. My knees bend to take the impact of each step. I imagine myself bolting past Neville O'Shea and reaching for the cheese. I picture Heather and Emily standing in the crowd, huge smiles on their faces as they clap and cheer. I can't help but grin as I visualise myself reaching for the cheese.

Whoosh!

The imaginary cheese shoots from my grasp. Heather and Emily's smiles vanish as Neville O'Shea scoops up the wheel.

My eyes fly open. 'That shouldn't happen!'

Visualising success has never been a problem before. It's helped me to win my four All-Australian jerseys. But unlike footy, chasing a cheese wheel down a steep slope in England is new to me.

I attempt to visualise myself racing again. I picture the cheese wheel spinning down the hill. I'm running side-by-side with Neville. I imagine him leaning into me, the feel of his bony shoulder jabbing into my ribs as he tries to knock me off balance. In my mind, I lower my centre of gravity and hustle forward. I picture the cheese flying towards the ledge. Forming a mental image of the cheese zipping forward, I prepare myself for it by extending my hands further away from my body.

Whack!

The imaginary cheese flies *up* off the ledge and clobbers me on the chin!

For the first time in my life I've been KO'd by an imaginary object. I need help.

'Hey, Boss,' I say into my mobile phone.

'Don't tell me you're in the Northern Territory competing in the Emu-Riding Rodeo!' yells Eddie. 'The only birds I want you sitting on the back of are the Crows players in three weeks.'

'It's not that, Eddie.' I get down to business. 'I'm working on visualising some game day stuff, but things keep going wrong upstairs.'

Eddie pauses like he's about to ask the million-dollar question on one of his game shows. 'Some footballers overthink the game. They play it too many times in their head before they take the field. It might be time you just turned up and backed yourself to get the job done on the day.'

'Cheers, Eddie.'

'We're talking about footy, aren't we, Steph?'

'What else is there?'

Hundreds of spectators line the sides of Cooper's Hill. Standing under the row of trees on either side of the hill, they eat sandwiches and sip cordial behind the orange and white plastic barriers separating them from the course.

'Hey! What are you doing?!' I shout, as Emily shakes Neville's hand.

Emily hurries over.

I put my hand on her shoulder. 'You told me Neville's dodgier than a mouldy mozzarella. Why would you shake his hand?'

Emily grins triumphantly. 'I've made a bet.'

My eyebrows shoot up, like a goal umpire raising the flags after a goal.

'Granny will quit making cheese if Neville wins this year's race,' explains Emily.

I feel my eyebrows shoot even higher, like a cricket umpire signalling a six.

'But when you win, it'll be Neville who

has to close down the cheese-making section of *his* business.'

My eyebrows can't go any higher, but my voice does. 'Me . . . win . . . Heather keeps her business?'

'I've got faith in you, Steph. You'll do just fine.' Heather grabs hold of my hand. I was so caught up in the conversation with Emily I didn't even notice she'd arrived.

'You know about the bet?'

'Emily suggested it. I thought it a splendid idea.'

I feel anything but splendid. A lump forms in my throat. I'm no longer just racing for a win, I'm also racing to save Heather's business!

Chapter 6

Years of playing footy has taught me that anything can happen in sport. Anyone can win. If I'm the reason Heather has to close her business it will be like missing a goal . . .

After the final siren . . .

In the grand final . . .

With my team down by five points.

'You've got to cancel the bet with Neville!' I say.

'Why the doubt? I've got confidence in you,' says Heather.

I wish I shared her confidence.

Emily seems even more confident than her grandmother. 'Wait till you see what we made, Steph.' She carefully places a basket at my feet.

Images of what the basket may contain flash through my brain. Maybe there's a new pair of boots in there that will help me speed down the hill. Or there could be gloves with spikes for gripping the cheese wheel. Right now, I'll take any help I can get.

I flip open the lid of the basket. What's in there surprises me more than a tag in the backline.

'A new football?' I try to hide my disappointment. Giving me a football is like giving an AFLW umpire a whistle. I've got more footballs than most people have pairs of socks. 'Thanks, but–'

'It's made from Double Gloucester,' says Emily. 'It's a cheese ball!'

'What? Why?'

'You'll be chasing this beauty down Cooper's Hill today,' says Heather. 'Kiss your troubles reading the bounce goodbye.'

'Really? You can do that?'

Heather winks at me. 'Neville's not the only one who can play tricks around here.'

I throw my arms around my new friends. 'This cheese ball is the best thing since sliced bread.'

'Don't you mean sliced cheese?' giggles Emily.

I grab the wax-coated cheese ball and study it. The dimensions are perfect. It's the same length as a footy. The same width. The cheese ball even has stitching in the seams and laces at the top. Sniffing the cheese ball near Heather's Double Gloucester logo, I wait for the leathery smell to fill my nostrils.

'Pwoah! It stinks like cheese!'

'It *is* cheese,' laughs Emily.

'Have a try of it, dear,' says Heather.

I motion to rip off the wax coating and bite into the cheese ball.

'No!' screams Emily, waving her arms.

'Have a try *chasing* it,' explains Heather.

Dropping the cheese ball to the ground, I tap it along in front of me, like I'm getting a feel for the footy before a big match. Every now and then I attempt to grab it, and I never fail to take it clean. I grip the cheese ball and visualise myself chasing it down Cooper's Hill. This time I have no problem imagining myself dashing down the slope and scooping up the cheese. I allow myself to dream of winning. I picture myself hugging Heather and Emily and whooping in the winner's photo, with Heather's Double Gloucester logo front and centre on the cheese ball.

'Good grief! A ball made from cheese?

That idea stinks worse than Collingwood's playing list,' sniggers Neville, snapping me back to reality. 'May I enquire as to where the cheese that I'll be winning today is?'

'Right here, bud.' I spin the cheese ball on one finger and point at it with a finger on my other hand.

'Protest! Protest!' Neville grabs Alex Fairbank, who is mid-conversation with another racer, and shoves him towards me. 'These scoundrels have created a cheese ball for the race. Tradition dictates that we chase a cheese wheel.'

Alex straightens his shirt and then rubs his hand on his chin. 'Heather, is this the cheese you intend to present for this year's race?'

'Yes. It's a Double Gloucester, as always.'

'Do the rules say it has to be wheel-shaped?' Emily asks the question, even though she's plainly researched the answer.

Fishing around in his pocket, Alex produces a rulebook.

'There's no need to check the rules, you buffoon,' protests Neville, gritting his teeth. 'This is cheating. I won't stand for it!'

Alex ignores the protests and flips through his rule book, muttering by-laws. 'In the case of mouldy cheese, lactose-intolerant competitors, reduced-fat cheese-chasing . . . hmm. I can find nothing in the rules detailing the shape of the cheese to be chased,' he announces. 'The cheese ball is therefore permitted.'

'Rubbish!'

Alex flips shut his rule book. 'The decision has been made,' he calls over his shoulder and walks back towards the competitor Neville tore him away from.

Neville storms after him, shouting. 'This is a travesty! It's cheating in the highest degree. Cheese-chasing is a noble pursuit. You're ruining years of tradition!'

'He's putting on a better tag than your best stopper at the Pies,' laughs Emily.

She's right. Neville is the first person I've met who'd give Eddie a run for his money in an argument.

'That's our part done,' says Heather. 'Time for you to do yours, missy.'

I give her a thumbs-up. 'With this cheese ball, it'll be a cakewalk.'

Chapter 7

At the start of the two-kilometre time trial we completed during Collingwood's preseason, I looked straight ahead and focussed on the track. Standing on the starting line of the Cooper's Hill Cheese-Rolling Race, I'm looking straight down. Not at my feet, but down the abrupt angle of Cooper's Hill. A group of burly rugby players stand at the bottom ready to catch us, because we'll build up so much speed running down the slope that we won't be able to stop by ourselves. The players' arms stick out like they're carrying a watermelon under each limb. A medical team waits nearby, the ambulance doors open and ready for injured racers.

Behind me, Neville O'Shea checks his gear one last time. Wiping dirt from a shovel, he packs his belongings back into a kitbag.

The spectators surge forward and lean against the barriers, yelling encouragement to their favoured racers.

'Go, Steph!' shouts Emily.

'Good luck, Steph,' calls Heather.

Neville barges his way next to me on the starting line. He pretends to pose for a winner's photo, smug look and all. 'Just giving you a preview of tomorrow's paper,' he says.

'May the cheese be with you, Steph!' calls Emily.

'May the what be where?!' snaps Neville.

There's doubt in his voice. I pounce on

the opportunity. 'The Double Gloucester cheese ball is a difficult chase. It can bounce up at some times and speed away at others.'

'I believe you'll find that Cooper's Hill is equally as challenging. It can be frightfully different from one day to the next.'

What? It's my turn to face doubt. Sure, footy ovals can change conditions when footy boots chop them up, or if the play is all on one side, but hills don't change much. Do they?

Alex Fairbank raises the microphone to his mouth. 'Ladies and gentlemen. It gives me great pleasure to announce that the time has arrived for the main event: the twenty-sixth annual Cooper's Hill Cheese-Rolling Race!'

The crowd's roar is almost as loud as when we ran onto Princes Park for the first ever game of AFLW.

'Racers, to receive the title of World Champion Cheese-Chaser, you must capture the Double Gloucester before any of your competitors,' says Alex. 'As is our custom, this year's winner will have the honour of taking home the Double Gloucester cheese wheel, pardon me, cheese ball, you will be pursuing.'

Most of the competitors turn and shake hands with the racers beside them.

A short, stocky man in a black T-shirt stands beside me. 'Best of luck,' I say as I shake his hand. Leaving my hand extended, I turn to Neville.

He continues to stare down the hill and ignores my offer.

'Safe travels,' announces Alex. 'On your marks! Get set!' He kneels and releases the cheese ball down the hill.

Pausing briefly, Alex allows the cheese

time to tumble end-over-end and gather speed.

'Go!'

Using my quick first step, like I'm pre-empting a forward's lead from the goal square, I jump to a good start. Neville, however, is already a step in front.

Bouncing on its point several times, the cheese ball darts to the left.

The racers that haven't already face-planted into Cooper's Hill gallop after it.

Suddenly, the ball jolts right.

Neville swerves and knocks the racer in the black T-shirt off-balance.

'Oomph!' The man thuds on the ground. He tumbles further down the hill, stopping his descent by latching onto a clump of grass and earth. He's not the only fallen competitor. In front of him other racers tumble and trip, leaving a trail of flailing and sliding bodies behind the leaders: Neville and me.

Neville closes in on the cheese.

I scramble behind him.

'It's mine!' Neville snatches at the cheese ball. If he gets it, Heather's business is doomed. I can only watch, and hope for a lucky bounce.

Thumping into the ground, the ball darts away from Neville's grasp and continues to tumble down the hill. I'd breathe a sigh of relief, but I'm too busy hurtling down the hill.

We're metres in front of the nearest racers, but only centimetres apart.

Whack!

Neville jabs his pointy elbow into my ribs.

'Give him one back, with interest!' calls Emily.

I don't flinch. 'That's all you've got? The Pies' junior mascots are bigger than you.'

The cheese chase continues.

Bang!

Neville darts sideways and delivers a hip-and-shoulder Eddie would be proud of.

Flying sideways, I'm forced to take several short steps to avoid plunging into the turf.

Neville gains several metres on me and grabs at the cheese ball.

Thwack!

The cheese ball slams into the ground and flies into the air, narrowly shooting through Neville's clasping hands.

Like a footy player sitting under a hospital pass, Neville steadies his feet, positions himself under the cheese ball and holds his arms out for the mark. He tilts his neck so his face points to the sky. 'I told you the best racer would prevail,' he calls.

Regathering my footing, I dash forward.

The cheese ball drops quickly, falling straight towards the mischievous midget's outstretched arms.

Heather thrusts her hands over her eyes.

'Barrel into him, Steph!' calls Emily. 'There's no match review panel in cheese-chasing!'

If I don't do something quickly, Neville will have another win . . . and Heather will be out of business.

Chapter 8

'Positioned under the falling cheese ball is Neville O'Shea,' Alex calls into the microphone. 'Unless the other racers get their act together, he'll be dining on Double Gloucester again this evening.'

Aside from Neville and me, only two other racers remain, well behind us. The rest have fallen, tumbled, toppled, or a combination of all three. I'm the only one with a hope of stopping him.

I hit my stride again as I pelt towards him. My coaches taught me to catch the ball at the highest possible point to keep opponents from spoiling the mark with a punch. Neville's arms are in front of him, ready to take a chest mark. It gives me a chance, and that's all I need.

Being a backline player means I'm experienced in this situation. Taking a giant stride towards Neville, I plant my left leg on the ground and launch into the air.

The cheese ball is centimetres above his head.

I form a fist with my right hand.

Thump!

As I drive my fist into the cheese ball, it flies off my knuckles and zooms downhill.

Slap!

Neville's hands slap onto his chest.

'If you're too slow and you know it, slap your chest!' shouts Emily.

I land and continue the cheese chase.

Neville takes off again, his thin legs pumping furiously, this time with the other two competitors beside him.

I'm five steps in front of the pack, speeding towards the bouncing cheese. Eyeing the ball, I try to pick my moment to lunge forwards and go for it.

'You little beauty!' I cheer.

A familiar landmark is nearby. The ledge I used in practice to catch my real footy should only be metres away. I know exactly what to do. Dashing around the side of the cheese ball, I stop metres in front of it, turn and hold my hands in front of my chest, ready for the ball to shoot into my waiting hands.

The cheese ball bounces a metre before the ledge.

It tumbles through the air.

The next bounce will be on the ledge.

Whack!

'What!?'

The cheese ball bounces where the ledge is, or used to be! In its place sits a patch of freshly turned dirt. Instead of shooting forward into my hands, the cheese ball launches straight into the air.

My mind flashes back to Neville's kitbag – and the dirty shovel! He's dug out the ledge because he's seen me use it in practice. Unbelievable! That's like the home team moving the goal posts seconds before the first bounce.

There's no time to sulk. I snap into action. Running in to a marking contest against the direction of the oncoming pack is the bravest thing you can do on a footy field, and one of the most dangerous. I've done it plenty of times before. Now it's time to put my body on the line again.

Neville and the two other competitors charge down the hill, their eyes focussing on the cheese ball as it sails through the sky.

I turn and dash back *up* the hill!

The cheese ball seems to pause in the air, before gravity takes effect and pulls it towards earth.

The three runners dashing downhill barge their way towards the drop zone; Neville slightly in front.

I hustle towards them.

The cheese ball continues to drop.

The three downhill runners launch in a tangle of arms and legs.

'It's yours, Steph!' calls Emily.

I leap with no thoughts for my safety. I soar through the air, full-chested towards the oncoming pack. My knee thuds on Neville's shoulder. It propels me even higher. My outstretched arms reach for the cheese ball.

'Steph Chiocci, you little beauty!' screams Alex into the microphone.

I squeeze the cheese ball in my hands, sail over Neville and land on my feet!

Chapter 9

'It gives me great pleasure in declaring the winner of the Cooper's Hill Cheese-Rolling Race to be Steph Chiocci!' cheers Alex into the microphone.

'You won!' cheers Emily, raising my arm in the air.

'You've saved my business!' says Heather.

'And you've taken the mark of the century,' adds Emily.

'Not bad for a footy player who's supposed to be resting,' I say.

Neville continues to stumble down

the hill. His mouth hanging open, he stares back over his shoulder at me as I embrace the cheese ball like it's the AFLW Premiership Cup.

Thump!

Neville's face slams into the rock-hard chest of a rugby player at the bottom of the hill. He collapses flat on his back.

The player grips Neville's shirt and pulls him to his feet in one swift movement.

Rubbing his head, Neville watches Heather, Emily and me celebrating with our arms draped over each other.

'You did it!' Emily wraps me in a bear hug.

'*We* did it!' I shout.

A photographer rushes in front of us. 'Say, um . . . erm . . . cheese?'

I thrust the cheese ball towards the camera and point enthusiastically at the Heather's Double Gloucester logo.

My English mates copy me.

'This will be seen from Gloucester to Collingwood!' I say.

Snap! *Click*!

The photographer fires off hundreds of snaps. Finally, she spins her camera around and flicks through her photos. 'Fabulous shots, but this one will go viral,' she says.

The digital screen lights up with a shot of me marking the cheese ball high above my head, one knee on the shoulder of Neville, facing in the opposite direction. Heather's logo shines on the ball.

'That'll sell truckloads of cheese!' cheers Emily.

'And you, Steph, have earned free cheese for the rest of your life,' says Heather.

Neville trudges up the hill, staring at his feet. He ignores my offer of a handshake.

'You were good,' calls Emily, 'but Steph was *feta*.'

I jog to the quarter-time huddle. We hold a fifteen-point lead over the Doggies. My opponent is scoreless and I've racked up twelve touches.

Eddie scuffs my hair. I let him get away with it, even though he'd be furious if I did the same to his. 'You're on fire, Steph! Those rest days really paid off.'

'Yeah, something like that.'

He pulls me aside. 'Do you know anything about this?' He grabs a newspaper clipping from the breast pocket of his jacket and holds it in front of me. The headline reads, 'Aussie Footy Hero Takes Screamer to Become Cheese-Chasing Champ'.

It's impossible for me not to smile. 'Sounds like a talented athlete. She must be a ripper.'

'She sure is,' says Eddie. 'Now how about you forget about these other sports and focus on footy?'

'I will,' I say – before muttering the rest of my reply under my breath. 'For the next three quarters.'

Steph Facts

Full Name: Stephanie Elizabeth Chiocci
Nicknames: Choch, Choo, Effie
Born: 06/12/1988
Height: 170cm
Footy Position: Midfield, Half Back
Footy Teams: Collingwood, Diamond Creek
Achievements:
- Pick 11 in the AFL Women's Draft: Collingwood Football Club (2016 – Present)
- Captain of the Collingwood Football Club Women's Team (2017 – Present)
- Member of AFL Victoria Women's

Academy (2015 – 2016)
- 3 x Diamond Creek Women's Football Club Best & Fairest (2006, 2012, 2016)
- Captain Diamond Creek Women's Football Club (2014 - Present)
- Western Bulldogs Women's Team Captain (2015 - 2016)
- Runner Up League Best & Fairest (2009, 2015)
- Pick 2 in the AFL Women's Draft to the Western Bulldogs (2013 - 2016)
- 4 x Senior Victorian Representative (2009, 2011, 2013, 2015)
- 4 x All Australian (2007, 2009, 2011, 2013)
- 7 x Victorian Metro Team (2007, 2009, 2010, 2011, 2012, 2013, 2014)
- Premier Division Premiership (2012)
- Diamond Creek Women's Football Club Team of the Decade Half Back Flank (2012)

- High Performance Academy (2010, 2012)
- 1 x Under 19 State Representative (2007)
- North West Division Premiership & Best on Ground in Grand Final (2006)
- Victorian Women's Football League Best First Year Player (2006)

Q: Did you always want to be a footy player?

I always loved football, but never thought I would be able to play. I watched my brothers play during their junior career and was always jealous that there was no girls' team for me to play in. I would have had to play against the boys if I wanted to play football when I was in primary school. I never did. I did, however, play in my grade six football team with the boys, and was the vice-captain!

Q: Which sports did you play growing up?

I was involved in Little Athletics, basketball and hockey. At school I made sure I participated in as many sports as possible including soccer, football and cricket. Lots of the skills and tactics from these sports can help with playing AFL.

Q: At what age did you start playing footy?

I started playing football at the age of seventeen. I went straight into a senior women's team as I wasn't aware there was a youth girls' competition!

Q: What do you think were the main reasons you made it to the highest level of your sport?

It comes down to work ethic and attitude. I knew I had some talent but talent alone doesn't get you very far these days. I worked really hard on my fitness and made sure

I listened to my coaches for feedback on how I could improve.

Q: What is the best thing about playing AFLW?

The fact that I get to play the best sport in the world with my teammates and that we are inspiring young female footballers to achieve their own dreams. Playing alongside my wonderful teammates and representing the biggest club in the country is so special. To have the support of all the supporters, men's players and all the staff at the club is also pretty amazing. I feel truly blessed to be a part of the Collingwood family. In the AFLW my favourite team to play against is Carlton as it is one of the oldest rivalries in the AFL.

Q: What is your favourite position to play?

It's in the midfield or as a high half forward. This means you can run into the midfield but then also try and kick goals!

Q: What advice do you have for young girls who want to play AFLW?

Keep working hard and listen to the feedback given to you; both positive and critical. Focus on the fundamentals of the game: kicking, handballing and marking, as these are the most important skills that will help you be a better player and potentially separate you from the others. Fitness and game sense will come as you get older. Susan Alberti once said, 'Never give up, never, ever, give up', and this is something that I live by. Work on your weaknesses and embrace your strengths, but most importantly, make sure you enjoy what you're doing!

Spoiling from Behind

When Neville is perched under the falling cheese it looks like he's going to win the race. That is, until I spoil with a booming punch from behind. The spoil from behind is a skill I often use to stop opposition forwards from marking. Follow these steps and you can do it, too!

1. Keep your eyes on the ball throughout the spoil.
2. Approach the ball as if you are going to try and mark it.
3. Leap off one foot, being careful not

to jump into your opponent's back.
4. Clench your fist and stretch your arm towards the path of the ball.
5. Punch the ball with your fist at the highest possible point, before your opponent has a chance to mark it.

TAKING A SCREAMER

I win the cheese race by taking the mark of the century over nasty Neville. There are not many better feelings in footy than sitting on someone's shoulders and hauling in a big mark. Here's how to do it:

1. Move forward to where you think you can meet the ball, always keeping your eyes focussed on your target.
2. Keep your body in line with the ball.
3. Leap off one foot while raising the knee on your opposite leg.
4. Rest your knee on your opponent's

back or shoulders.
5. Reach towards the ball with your fingers stretched and the tips of your thumbs touching.
6. Let the ball come to you, absorbing the force of the ball in your hands and supporting the ball from behind with your thumbs.
7. Celebrate taking Mark of the Year!

More great reading from Ford Street Publishing

HAZARD RIVER
SHARK FRENZY!

Jack Wilde and his friends are on holidays at Hazard River when they discover a dead shark washed up on the sand. It has no fins. Is it the work of a monster shark ... a giant squid ... or pirates? The gang decides to investigate. But finding out what killed the shark lands the kids in a whole lot of trouble.

J.E. FISON

www.fordstreetpublishing.com

FORD ST

More great reading from Ford Street Publishing

THE VANILLA SLICE KID

Adam Wallace and Jack Wodhams
Illustrations by Tom Gittus

Archie Cunningham is a shy boy who has three things – incredibly mean and greedy parents, no friends, and an amazing power.

When an uploaded video shows the world what Archie can do, he suddenly becomes the main ingredient in a recipe for world domination.

And then the fun really begins!

www.fordstreetpublishing.com

FORD ST